Words to Know Before You Read

Appaloosa
candidate
election
elephant
giraffe
hippopotamus
lizard
organize
raccoon

www.rourkeeducationalmedia.com

Edited by Precious McKenzie
Illustrated by Marc Mones
Art Direction and Page Layout by Renee Brady

Library of Congress PCN Data

Vote for Me! / J. Jean Robertson
ISBN 978-1-61810-183-9 (hard cover) (alk. paper)
ISBN 978-1-61810-316-1 (soft cover)
Library of Congress Control Number: 2012936784

Rourke Educational Media
Printed in the United States of America,
North Mankato, Minnesota

rourkeeducationalmedia.com

customerservice@rourkeeducationalmedia.com   •   PO Box 643328 Vero Beach, Florida 32964

Vote for Me!

By J. Jean Robertson
Illustrated by Marc Mones

It was that time of the year again, election time. As the former class president, Penelope Pony had to make an announcement to her fellow classmates.

Penelope Pony said, "Class, I need your attention. It is time for our class to organize and elect new officers. We'll begin with class president."

"You may decorate the halls with posters which tell why you should be president."

OR A CLASS PRESIDENT
WHO IS HEADS
ABOVE EVERYONE
VOTE FOR ME!
GERRY GIRAFFE
FOR PRESIDENT.
ELECT A PRESIDENT
YOU CAN LOOK UP TO

5

"Helga, did you hear? We get to make posters for elections in art class today."

"That is wonderful, Zoe. We can help each other."

"Helga and Zoe, you are a great team!"

"The students who are not running for office may volunteer to help a candidate."

IF YOU WANT A PRESIDENT WHO WILL NEVER LET YOU DOWN VOTE FOR ME! HELP ELVIN ELEPHANT WIN THE ELECTION. I CAN CARRY THE LOAD.

9

"We should, Amber, because our teacher gave us the whole afternoon for this project."

"I will need a ladder to hang my poster."

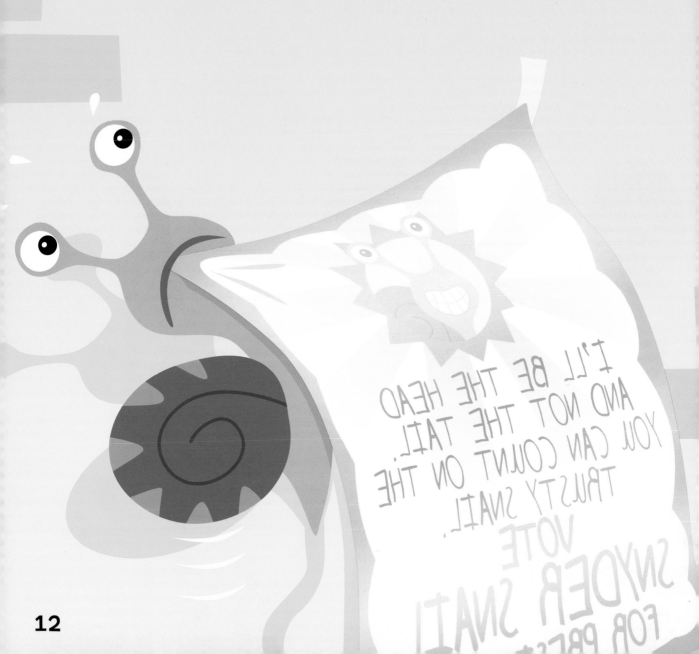

"No you won't, Snyder. With my long neck, I can reach it for you."

"Elvin, do you have the materials you need to finish your poster?"

"No, Penelope. I need more markers to finish."

"Lena, could you please share the markers with Elvin and me?"

"Zoe, your poster looks finished, so I have a job for you."

VOTE FOR
ZOE ZEBRA
FOR CLASS PRESIDENT!
YOU CAN TELL BY
EACH LOVELY STRIPE,
I'LL BE A LEADER
OF THE FINEST TYPE.

"Please go to the office and ask Ms. Mitten for enough tape to hang the posters in the hall."

"Thank you, Zoe. Good job!"

"Now, let's get these posters hung in the hall."

Tomorrow's the day, voting day! Cast your vote! Whoever wins, it will be O.K.

Who will our new president be? If you stop by the school tomorrow at three, you will see.

After Reading Activities

You and the Story...

Which one of the animals would you vote for?

Why would you vote for that one?

List three things that would help someone be a good class president.

What would you do if you were class president?

Words You Know Now...

Notice the six sets of double letters in these words. On a piece of paper, write four new words using the same double letters found in these words.

Appaloosa	hippopotamus
candidate	lizard
election	organize
elephant	raccoon
giraffe	

You Could...Pretend You Are Running For Class President

- List three things about you that would help you be a good class president.

- Ask several classmates to tell you what they think a good president would do.

- Ask an adult what they think a good president would do.

- Make a poster to help you get votes in a class election.

- Write an acceptance speech to give in case you win.

- Describe how you would support the new class president if someone else won.

About the Author

J. Jean Robertson, also known as Bushka to her grandchildren and many other kids, lives in San Antonio, Florida with her husband. She is retired after many years of teaching. She loves to read, travel, and write books for children.

Ask The Author!
www.rem4students.com

About the Illustrator

Marc Mones is a Spanish illustrator. He lives in Bolvir, a small town in the Pyrenees, with his wife Rose, his two sons Gerard and Martin, and his four cats. Marc has liked to draw since he was a little kid. His father is also an illustrator and his mother is a very good painter. His very favorite things to draw are monsters!

CSCL

DATE DUE

NOV 24 2015		
FEB 03 2016		
FEB 17 2016		
NOV 14 2016		
FEB 06 2017		
GAYLORD		PRINTED IN U.S.A.